MW01051277

DISCOVERY & INVENTIONS

DISCOVERY & INVENTIONS

Geoff Endacott

Viking

VIKING
Published by the Penguin Group
Viking Penguin Inc., 375 Hudson Street,
New York, NY 10014, U.S.A.
Penguin Books Ltd, 27 Wrights Lane,
London W8 5TZ, England
Penguin Books Australia Ltd, Ringwood,
Victoria, Australia
Penguin Books Canada Ltd, 2801 John Street,
Markham, Ontario, Canada L3R 1B4
Penguin Books (N.Z.) Ltd, 182–190 Wairau Road,
Auckland 10, New Zealand

Penguin Books Ltd, Registered Offices:
Harmondsworth, Middlesex, England

First published in 1991 by Viking Penguin, a division of
Penguin Books U.S.A.

**STRANGE & AMAZING WORLDS:
DISCOVERY & INVENTIONS**
was conceived, edited and designed by
Marshall Editions
170 Piccadilly
London W1V 9DD

Copyright © Marshall Editions Developments Limited
1991
All rights reserved

Editor: Fran Jones
Design: Millions Design
Picture Research: Dee Robinson
Editorial Research: Jazz Wilson, Sean Callery
Editorial Director: Ruth Binney
Production: Barry Baker
Janice Storr
Nikki Ingram

Library of Congress catalog card number: 91-50210
(CIP data available)

ISBN 0-670-84177-3

Typeset by MS Filmsetting Limited, Frome, Somerset
Originated in Hong Kong by
Regent Publishing Services Ltd
Printed and bound in Spain
by Artes Graficas, Toledo
D.L.TO:937–1991

10 9 8 7 6 5 4 3 2 1

Contents

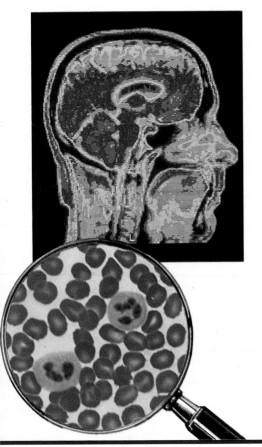

Introduction

The world of discovery and inventions is full of strange and amazing stories. These are stories of luck and accidents, of ingenuity and imagination – and tales of sheer genius. Who would believe, for example, that a child's illness could have led to the invention of the pneumatic tire, that the "passengers" in the first-ever balloon flight were a sheep, a rooster and a duck, or that television was made possible with the help of some knitting needles and a hatbox?

Behind every great discovery and invention is a human mind set alight by a spark of inspiration. But the time and place also have to be right for an inventor's dreams to become reality. Leonardo da Vinci created designs for an airplane, a helicopter, a submarine, and a parachute, none of which was actually made until more than 400 years after he first drew them.

In the 1830s, Charles Babbage worked out how to make mathematical calculations using an "analytical engine," but it took another 100 years to build a computer that could do the job he had in mind. By wondering what it might be like to travel on a beam of light Albert Einstein was led to his theory of relativity.

Success does not always arrive instantly, however. Robert Goddard, inventor of the rocket, saw his first attempts fail as his liquid-fueled rocket landed in his aunt's

garden. Austrian monk Gregor Mendel spent some 25 years painstakingly experimenting with garden peas in order to discover the basic laws of inheritance. Courage, too, can be a vital ingredient. Without daring to risk a child's life to prove his theory of vaccination, Edward Jenner would never have made the breakthrough which ultimately resulted in a victory over smallpox. Bravery was undoubtedly necessary for the conquest of the air, demonstrated by pioneers of flight such as the Montgolfier brothers and their fellow Frenchman, Louis Blériot.

Chance can also play an amazing part in progress: Alexander Fleming's unexpected find of mold on one of his experiments led to the discovery of penicillin; Wilhelm Roentgen accidentally discovered X-rays while trying to find out what happens when electricity is passed through a gas; and modern photography began when Louis Daguerre chanced on the fact that a hidden image could be stored on a plate of copper coated with silver iodide.

The inventiveness of the human mind is truly amazing. In this book you will find just a few of the most astounding stories that have helped shape the world we live in.

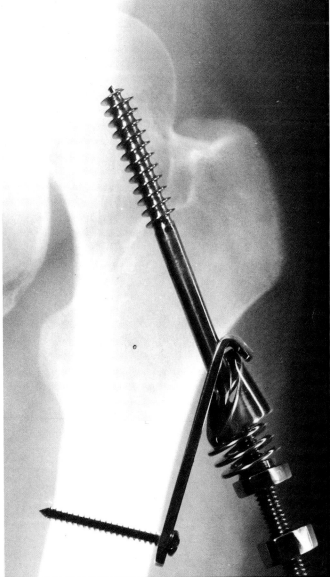

THE PRINTED WORD

The Chinese first developed printing 3,000 years ago. Words and letters were cut into stones which were inked and pressed onto paper to make an image. The Chinese also invented moveable type, where the letters were cut out individually and moved around to form different words, like a game of Scrabble.

This took a lot of time, but the process was speeded up with the first printing press, built by a German inventor, Johannes Gutenberg. His machine had a plate, or "bed," of metal type, with each letter fixed in a block of wood. Another part of the press was a moveable flat piece of wood called a platen. Ink was put on the type, paper placed on top, and the platen screwed down over it. Gutenberg could now print more reading material in a day than a scribe could copy in a year. He began by printing 200 copies of the Bible

Today, computers do much of the work of printing. Words are entered into a computer program, which can then design how each page will look. This image is transferred onto a transparent film from which printing plates are made.

▲ This laborious method was used to produce books before printing was available. Scribes would spend weeks producing a single book, copying from the original by hand.

▲ In 1455, Gutenberg's Bible was the first book to be printed on a printing press.

THE PEN'S PROGRESS

From the earliest times quill pens, made from reeds or bird feathers, were used for writing. The first practical fountain pen was produced by an American, L. E. Waterman, in 1844, and made writing much faster.

Some analysts think handwriting may reveal details of a person's character. The high letters in George Washington's signature are thought to show great idealism, and the fast but well-formed writing of Albert Einstein shows a quick mind, eager to be understood.

► *Newspapers have to be printed at high speed. The fastest presses can print over 30,000 copies in an hour. This press is at Trenton, New Jersey.*

FACT FILE

In the 1600s, metal type letters were made using molds called dies. Letters were reversed, (cast ''back to front'') to make them look correct when printed.

Photography and printing came together in the 1860s when a light-sensitive paper was invented. When this paper was pressed onto metal plates of type, the words became ''fixed.''

The world's fastest press can print all 773,692 words of the Bible in 65 seconds.

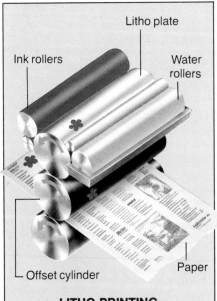

Litho plate

Ink rollers

Water rollers

Offset cylinder

Paper

LITHO PRINTING
Most modern printing uses a process called offset lithography. The image is formed photographically on a cylindrical plate. Ink sticks only to the parts which are to be printed.

► *Desktop publishing became popular during the 1980s. Pages are designed on a computer and printed out by a laser printer.*

MASTER MATHEMATICIAN

A visit to the public baths helped the Greek mathematician Archimedes to solve one of his toughest questions. King Hieron II wanted to know if his new crown was made of pure gold. When Archimedes stepped into a full bath, water spilled out – and gave him an idea. According to legend, he ran home naked, shouting "Eureka" ("I've found it").

He weighed the crown and measured how much water it displaced – what its "volume" was. He then determined the volume of a piece of pure gold of the same weight. Since the gold's volume was less, he proved that the crown was not pure. This discovery became known as Archimedes' Principle.

Archimedes solved other problems, too. He invented a pump to raise much-needed water up to dry land for farmers. This was a spiral fitted very tightly into a cylinder which pulled water up when it was turned.

He also discovered that when the distance around the outside of a circle (circumference) is divided by the length of the line passing through the circle's center (diameter), the result is always the same. He called this number "pi," the sixteenth letter of the Greek alphabet, π.

▶ *This machine is pulling up water from a stream. Called the Archimedes' screw, it was invented by him more than 2,000 years ago and is still an important tool for irrigating land.*

▶ *A compound pulley enables a small force to lift a heavy load. The hook on this crane is attached to a compound pulley. Archimedes' work on mechanics included a description of pulleys.*

ARCHIMEDES

287 B.C.: Archimedes was born in Syracuse, on the island of Sicily, the son of an astronomer and a relative of King Hieron II.

260–240 B.C.: Made a number of mathematical discoveries, built a planetarium, and experimented with levers.

215 B.C.: The Romans attacked Syracuse. Archimedes made the soldiers polish their shields so the reflected rays from the Sun set fire to the Roman ships.

212 B.C.: Archimedes was killed by a Roman soldier.

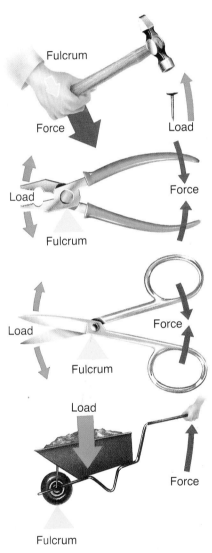

▼ Archimedes developed the theory of levers, simple but effective machines. A small force applied at one end of a lever can produce a large force in the opposite direction to the load. The fulcrum is the point or support on which the lever turns or moves.

Fulcrum

Force

Load

Load

Fulcrum

Force

Load

Force

Fulcrum

Load

Force

Fulcrum

◀ Supertankers need huge propellers to power them through the water. Ships' propellers use the same basic principle as an Archimedes' screw.

GENIUS AT WORK

How many school subjects are you good at? Leonardo da Vinci was very good at everything, especially art, music, math, and science.

The drawings of Leonardo, the greatest inventor of his day, include designs for an airplane, a helicopter, a submarine, a bicycle, and a parachute. He was a brilliant man, although not all of his designs would have worked in practice.

Like many artists, Leonardo was left-handed, but he wrote in mirror writing to conceal his ideas from jealous rivals. He was also such a perfectionist that many of his works were never finished. His most famous painting is the *Mona Lisa*, which took him four years to complete.

Leonardo was fascinated by the human body, and he learned a great deal by cutting up more than 30 dead bodies to examine them. He also loved practical jokes, and his notes include instructions on how to make stink bombs.

LEONARDO DA VINCI

1452: Leonardo da Vinci was born on April 15 in Vinci, Italy, the son of a lawyer and a peasant girl.

1482: Moved to Milan and became State Engineer.

1484: Milan struck by plague. Leonardo started work on town planning, believing this could reduce the spread of disease.

1497: Invented lock gates for canals. The first set of gates was installed in the Naviglio Interno Canal near Milan.

1499: French army invaded Milan and Leonardo was forced to flee.

1502: Became architect and engineer to Cesare Borgia, the son of Pope Alexander VI.

1516: Left Italy and settled in France at Château Cloux, near Amboise, to live as a guest of King François I.

1519: Died on May 2.

LEONARDO VINCI

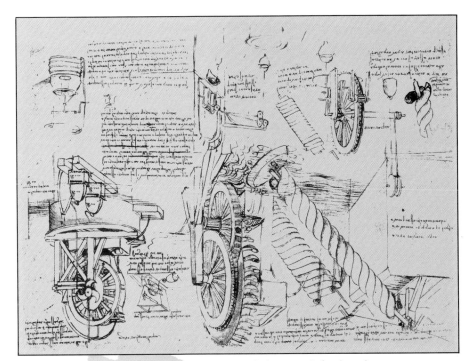

▲ Leonardo's drawings were incredibly detailed and showed an understanding of mechanics which was far ahead of his time. Unfortunately, he had no means of powering his inventions. The only available power supplies were water, horses, and human muscles.

◄ Among Leonardo's drawings are designs for a bicycle, a parachute, and a flying machine. None of them was ever built.

▲ This flying machine was built from a Leonardo da Vinci design, for an exhibition held in the 1980s. Although it could never have flown, it shows that Leonardo understood the basic rules of aerodynamics 400 years before the Wright brothers made their famous first flight.

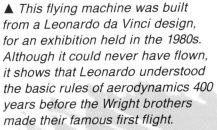

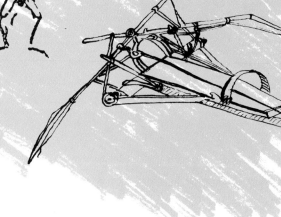

THE REVOLUTION OF THE EARTH

The Earth moves around the Sun. This is accepted as a fact today, but 500 years ago, everybody believed that our planet, not the Sun, was the center of the universe. Our modern understanding of how the Earth moves comes from the work of four important men.

In 1543 the Polish astronomer Copernicus published his book *Concerning the Revolution of the Celestial Spheres*. It was the first time anyone had said that the Earth revolved around the Sun.

Copernicus's ideas were supported by Galileo, who in 1610 used a telescope to show that the planet Jupiter had four satellites in orbit around it. This proved that some things did not orbit the Earth – contrary to the teachings of the Catholic church.

However, Galileo was not alone in his views. After his death, Johannes Kepler produced a set of mathematical laws to show that the Earth and other planets orbit around the Sun in ellipses, which are like flattened circles.

The English scientist Sir Isaac Newton finally explained that the planets are kept in orbit by the force of gravity.

▶ *Galileo shows the satellites of Jupiter to the political leaders in Venice. They could see the satellites moving around Jupiter, but many refused to believe it.*

▲ *This photograph was taken at Siding Spring in Australia. The camera shutter was left open for more than ten hours. The stars were spread out into curved "trails" as the Earth turned on its axis while moving around the Sun. The wavy line around the telescope dome was caused by a man holding a flashlight.*

GALILEO GALILEI

1564: Galileo Galilei was born on February 15 in Pisa, Italy.

1592: Discovered the basic principle of the pendulum.

1593: Designed a thermoscope to measure air temperature.

1610: Used his telescope to discover sunspots, craters on the Moon, and the four major satellites of Jupiter.

1632: Published *Dialogues on the Two Chief Systems of the World*. The Pope condemned his ideas, and all books were removed from circulation.

1642: Died on January 8.

▲ *These five photographs show a total eclipse of the Moon, step by step. A lunar eclipse occurs when the Moon passes through the Earth's shadow. The Moon is still lit during an eclipse because the atmosphere bends the Sun's light around the Earth.*

▲ *Galileo showed that "gravity pulls all bodies equally, regardless of their weight". This experiment was repeated on the Moon, where there is no air, using a hammer and a feather.*

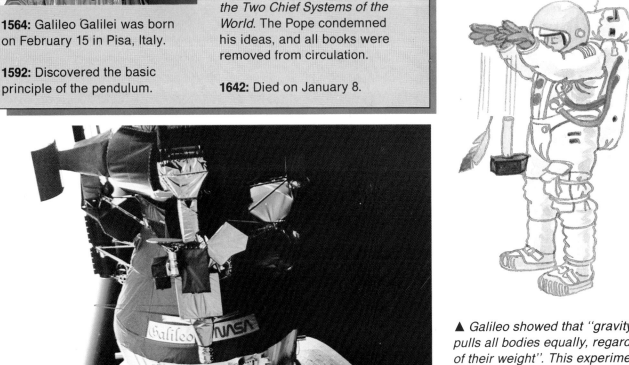

◄ *This NASA spacecraft is named* Galileo. *It was launched by the space shuttle* Atlantis *in October 1989 and will enter orbit around Jupiter in December 1995.*

THE WATER CLOSET

The first "water closet" was used during the reign of Queen Elizabeth I of England (1558–1603). Her godson, Sir John Harington, was thrown out of the royal court for telling a vulgar story. As he had liked the luxury of the royal palace, he had a grand house built. After 1589, this house featured his latest invention, a flushing toilet.

The queen forgave Sir John and visited him in 1592, when she became the first British monarch to use a water closet. Sir John was so pleased with his water closet that he wrote a book about it, boasting that he had one and the queen did not. Nevertheless, in 1597 a toilet was installed in her palace at Richmond, near London.

Toilets were still rare, however. Most people continued to use a hole in the ground. Whatever method was used, sewage was collected in a large hole called a cesspit.

The first widely used toilet was produced in the 1770s in London by Alexander Cummings. In 1857, American Joseph Gayetty made using a toilet much more pleasant when he invented toilet paper.

Sanitary engineer Thomas Crapper (1837–1910) perfected a toilet flush tank which discharged a large amount of water at high speed.

◀ Monasteries were among the first places to have toilets, as can be seen from this example of a medieval latrine.

◀ This toilet seat is fitted with chariot wheels and dates from the 2nd century A.D.

▲ This is the luxury version of the Macfarlane's Patent toilet – the basic model did not have the wood-covered seat or such a large hole!

▶ This luxury john dates from 1908, and has a Dresden pattern bowl, mahogany seat, and brass fittings.

▼ Bathrooms can be decorated in a wide variety of styles, but how many people would want to live like this?

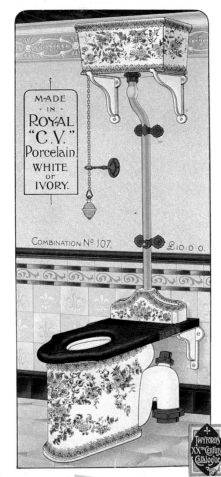

MADE IN ROYAL "C.V." Porcelain. WHITE or IVORY.

COMBINATION No 107. £10.0.0.

TWYFORDS XXᵀᴴ Century Catalogue

▼ Early toilet bowls were highly decorated, like this "raised oak" pattern in blue and white.

◀ When San Francisco jeweler Sidney Mobell decided to decorate his toilet seat, this is what he ended up with. The $260,000 seat is plated with 24-carat gold. The crown under the lid contains 160 sapphires, 137 rubies, 16 diamonds, 14 pearls, 8 emeralds, 7 amethysts, 5 garnets and 2 moonstones.

THE FIGHT AGAINST DISEASE

Modern medicine can protect you from disease and help you get better when you are ill. But 200 years ago, people could die in a few days if they became ill.

The first medical breakthrough was made by English physician Edward Jenner. In 1796, he injected an eight-year-old boy with cowpox, and six weeks later with smallpox – a dangerous disease. The boy did not become ill, because the first shot had protected him. Jenner, however, did not understand why his injection had worked.

In 1865, a French chemist, Louis Pasteur, wrote a paper that said the air was filled with invisible microbes that might be capable of carrying disease and infecting people.

An English surgeon, Joseph Lister, found this idea very interesting. Many of his patients were dying from infected wounds, and Pasteur's discovery made him realize that germs in operating rooms were causing the deaths. He invented an antiseptic spray of carbolic acid that could kill germs in the air.

Antibiotics kill germs, called bacteria, in the body. The first antibiotic was discovered by Alexander Fleming in 1928. Mold from a plant blew onto a dish containing bacteria. A blue-green mold (penicillin) started to grow and killed the bacteria. The fight against disease had really begun.

▶ Penicillin is extracted from the mold Penicillium notatum. Alexander Fleming discovered penicillin when the mold contaminated an experiment.

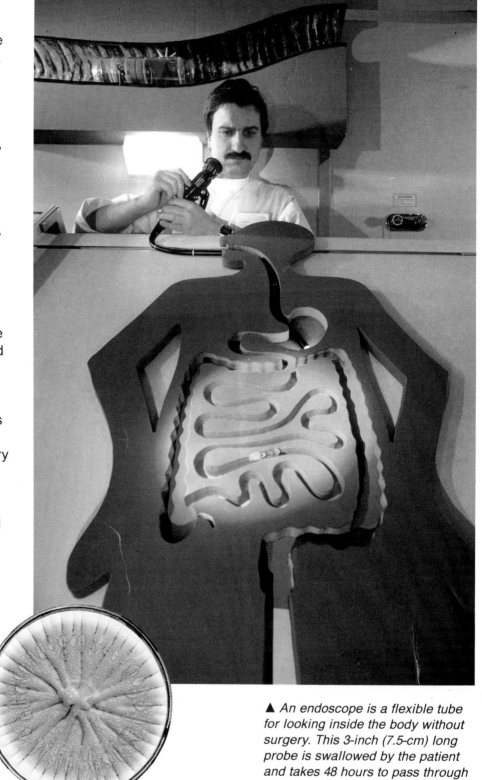

▲ An endoscope is a flexible tube for looking inside the body without surgery. This 3-inch (7.5-cm) long probe is swallowed by the patient and takes 48 hours to pass through the body. A tiny radio transmitter sends information about the small intestine as the probe passes through it.

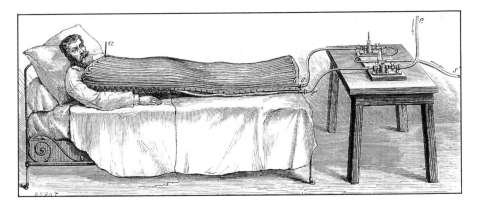

◄ Thank goodness we do not have to put up with this any more. The old picture shows an early attempt to refrigerate a patient to lower his temperature. The normal human body temperature is 98.4°F (36.9°C), but it can rise and cause a fever if you are ill. That is why a physician may want to take your temperature. A rise in body temperature to more than 106°F (41°C) can be extremely dangerous.

FACT FILE

Doctors of the late 19th century discovered that, just by washing their hands and disinfecting their clothes, they could prevent women from dying of infections when they were giving birth.

In the 1950s, many children died or were crippled by polio. Thanks to Jonas Salk, who discovered how to make a polio vaccine, we can be protected from the disease.

Christiaan Barnard brought hope for millions when he performed the first human heart transplant in 1967.

Chimpanzees use medicine, too. When they are ill, they chew the leaves of a plant called *Aspilia*, which are thought to contain an antibiotic.

The first wire sutures were invented in 1820 by French surgeon Pierre-François Percy.

▲ Based on work done by Louis Pasteur in the 1860s, milk is now heat-treated (pasteurized) to destroy any dangerous bacteria.

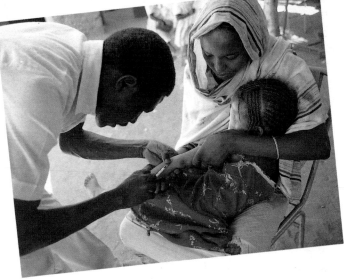

▲ Vaccination has made a lot of progress since Jenner's day. Jenner did not have syringes, so he used thorns to vaccinate people.

THE GENE MACHINE

When you look at people in the same family, you often notice that they look similar. Perhaps a son has the same-shaped nose as his mother and the same color eyes as his father. Physical features like these are determined by genes.

Our understanding of the way features are handed down from parents to children began with the work of an Austrian monk, Gregor Mendel (1822–84). He experimented by breeding peas and other plants in the garden of his monastery.

In this century, scientists have discovered that genes are found in chromosomes. Every cell in every human being has 46 chromosomes, 23 inherited from the mother and 23 from the father. Chromosomes are made from a chemical called DNA, which is shaped like two spirals twisted together. The shape of DNA was discovered in 1953 by an Englishman, Francis Crick,

GREGOR MENDEL

working with an American, James Watson.

Today, the characteristics of animals and plants can be changed by altering their DNA. This process is called genetic engineering. It has already been used to produce sheep whose milk contains medicines for humans.

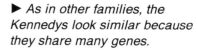

▶ As in other families, the Kennedys look similar because they share many genes.

▼ In peas the gene for tallness (T) is "dominant" over that for shortness (t) so that the Tt combination gives tall plants. Only tt gives short plants.

Tall parent

Short parent

TT

t t

Tall offspring

Tt

Tt

▲ There are about 400 different breeds of dogs. The differences between them are due to genes.

▶ The fruit fly breeds rapidly and is often used for genetic experiments.

American scientist Thomas Hunt Morgan performed many of his genetic experiments with fruit flies. In 1933 he was awarded a Nobel Prize for his discoveries about inheritance.

Every cell in every human contains about 100,000 genes.

If the DNA within a single human cell was stretched to its full length, it would be 6 feet (2 meters) long.

Genetic engineering can produce "clones" – plants and animals which have identical genes.

▶ DNA "fingerprints" can be used to prove whether or not people are related. The genetic information can be extracted from samples of blood.

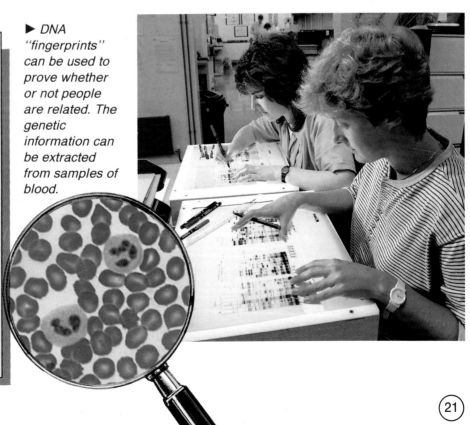

BUILDING BRIDGES

When Isambard Kingdom Brunel built an arched bridge over the River Thames, west of London, in 1838, his critics said it could never carry the weight of a train. It did – and is still being used 150 years later.

There are three main types of bridge: the beam bridge, whose weight is carried by supports at intervals along the bridge; the arch bridge, whose weight is carried at the two ends of the arch; and the suspension bridge, whose weight is carried mostly by the cables attached to the river banks.

The Romans first developed the art of bridge building, using stone blocks wedged against each other to form an arch. Variations of this were used until 1779, when the world's first iron bridge arched across the River Severn in England.

By the 1800s, cement and mass-produced steel could be used to provide greater strength. In 1874, James B. Eads made use of this technology and built the first steel bridge in St. Louis, Missouri.

▼ The first iron bridge was built at Coalbrookdale, England, by Abraham Darby in 1779. It spans 100 feet (30 meters).

▲ The Tarr Steps cross the River Barle in Somerset, England. Many of these "clapper" bridges are thousands of years old.

▶ The Pont du Gard aqueduct near Nîmes in France was built 2,000 years ago. It is 160 feet (49 meters) high and carries water across a valley.

FACT FILE

The Sumerians knew how to build arch bridges. They built one across the River Nile in 2650 B.C.

Scottish engineer Thomas Telford built 1,200 bridges. His best-known is the suspension bridge across the Menai Strait in Wales, completed in 1825.

Sydney Harbor Bridge, opened in 1932, was designed to carry four rail lines and a 57-foot (17-meter) wide road. It was tested by 72 locomotives weighing 7,600 tons.

The world's longest suspension bridge crosses the River Humber in England. It is so long, at 4,625 feet (1,410 meters), that designers had to allow for the curve of the Earth's surface when they were planning it.

▶ The Royal Albert Bridge across the River Tamar at Saltash, England, carries the main rail line from Plymouth to Penzance. It was designed by Isambard Kingdom Brunel, has two spans of 455 feet (139 meters), and is 100 feet (30 meters) above the water.

◀ The road deck of a suspension bridge hangs from cables. The 4,200-foot (1,280-meter) long Golden Gate Bridge in San Francisco was completed in 1937. Each of its main cables is 37 inches (94 cm) in diameter and contains 27,000 separate strands of wire.

▶ ELECTRICITY

Electricity is an immensely powerful form of energy. We can see it, as lightning, and can also turn it on at the flick of a switch. Without it, most of us could not light our homes, cook, or keep ourselves warm.

Although electricity does occur in nature, we can make it too. For this we can thank, among others, British scientist Michael Faraday (1791–1867). One of ten children, he became errand boy to a bookbinder when he was fourteen to help his family. But in addition to delivering the books, he read them. His studies led him to experiment with electricity,

which was then little understood.

Faraday's opportunity to develop his ideas came when he was made laboratory assistant to a chemist, Sir Humphrey Davy, in 1812. By experimenting with wire and magnets, Faraday discovered in 1831 that, when a magnet was moved in and out of a coil of wire, an electric current was created.

The electricity we use today is produced by huge generators in power stations. They burn coal, oil, or other fuels to drive turbines, which spin coils through magnets. This energy is sent along power lines to homes, offices, and factories.

▲ *Just imagine how big a flashlight would be if it were powered by one of these. This early chemical battery is called Volta's pile. It was built in 1799 by Italian physicist Alessandro Volta.*

▶ *There are so many electric lights in towns and cities that it never really gets dark. This is New York – the first city to be lit by Edison's electric light.*

▲ *In 1752 Benjamin Franklin showed that electricity occurs naturally, by flying a kite during a thunderstorm. Electricity traveled along the wet string of the kite to a key tied to the end.*

◀ *A streak of lightning is typically 4 miles (6 km) long, but can stretch up to 20 miles (32 km). The powerful electrical discharge travels at 87,000 miles per second (140,000 km/sec), which is nearly half the speed of light.*

Television

Stereo
system

Transformer

Refrigerator

Computer

Vacuum
cleaner

◀ A transformer
converts
electricity into
the right form. It
can then be
used to supply
homes and
offices.

▶ Electricity
can be made
using the Sun's
energy. This
French solar
power station
has 9,500
mirrors, each
18 inches
(45 cm) square.

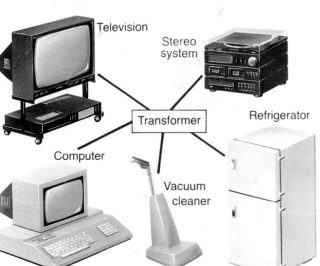

THE RECORDING MACHINE

"Genius is one percent inspiration and ninety-nine percent perspiration." Those were the words of Thomas Alva Edison, the most inventive man the world has ever known. Edison and his colleagues obtained patents for 1,093 inventions.

Despite his obvious success in later life, Edison had a difficult time at school and was eventually thrown out. The ten-year-old Thomas then set up his own laboratory at home.

Of all his inventions, Edison's own favorite was a machine to record sound called the phonograph. A drum covered in tinfoil was turned by hand. As it turned, and a person spoke, a sharp needle scratched the sound pattern into the surface of the foil. The first recording was the nursery rhyme *Mary Had a Little Lamb*. It was greeted with amazement, and Edison was called the Wizard of Menlo Park, where he had his laboratory.

His reputation led New York businessmen to advance him $30,000 to solve the problem of creating "electric" light. On December 3, 1879, he was able to demonstrate the first electric lamp.

THOMAS ALVA EDISON

1847: Thomas Alva Edison born on February 11 in Milan, Ohio.

1871: Invented the printing telegraph.

1877: Made the first sound recording machine, the phonograph.

1879: Created the first electric filament lamp, which burned for 45 hours.

1882: New York became the first town in the world to use electric light. The crowds cheered with excitement.

1931: Died on October 18, in West Orange, New Jersey.

▶ Talking dolls came into the shops during the 1890s. Each doll contained a tiny Edison phonograph.

▶ This label shows a dog named Nipper listening to "His Master's Voice" on an early record player. The photograph is still used today and will be recognized by anyone who buys recordings.

▲ This complex equipment was needed to record someone playing a piano in 1889.

▲ Early record players, like this Pathé Orpheus, had to be wound up by turning a handle. Sometimes the machine had to be rewound before the end of a record. Volume was controlled by opening or closing the doors.

▶ The first jukebox was installed in San Francisco by Louis Glass in 1899. Jukeboxes became a common sight during the 1940s. From 1946 to 1947, a total of 56,000 Wurlitzer Model 1015 jukeboxes were built.

SPACE SAVER
A single compact disc (CD) can store up to 74 minutes of stereo music on one side. Early vinyl records were 12 in (30 cm) in diameter, and each side played just four minutes of mono sound. That means nearly eighteen records would be needed to store the same information as a single CD.

RADIO WAVES

The sounds we hear from radios come through the air in the form of radio waves. The fact that magnetic waves of electricity travel invisibly through space at almost 186,000 miles per second (300,000 km/sec) was discovered by German physicist Heinrich Hertz in 1886.

A young Italian, Guglielmo Marconi, was inspired to try to send messages using these waves. His first success was to send a spark from a transmitter at one end of a table to a metal ring at the other end. He then built a bigger transmitter and sent signals in Morse code. He was thrilled when the receiver picked up and successfully repeated his signals. Marconi had, in fact, invented the first system of "wireless" telegraphy.

The Italian government, however, was not impressed with his work, and he moved to England, where he was encouraged to try sending messages across the water. By 1901, Marconi had successfully sent radio signals from Cornwall, England, to Newfoundland, Canada. By 1906, it was possible to transmit human speech.

Regular radio broadcasts began in the 1920s, although radios had to be large in order to hold all the equipment.

GUGLIELMO MARCONI

1874: Guglielmo Marconi born on April 25 in Bologna, Italy.

1894: Began radio experiments.

1899: Morse code radio message transmitted across the English Channel from Dover, England, to Wimereux, France.

1901: Message transmitted across the Atlantic Ocean from Cornwall, England, to Newfoundland, Canada.

1909: Awarded the Nobel Prize for Physics.

1937: Died on July 20 from a heart attack. The world observed a two-minute radio silence in his honor.

▲ Marconi's early experiments took place at his parents' home in Italy. The grounds were more than 1 mile (1.6 km) long, and Marconi eventually sent a radio signal from one end to the other.

▼ Communication satellites relay radio signals from one side of the Earth to the other. Their orbit, 22,900 miles (36,900 km) above the equator, keeps them over a fixed point on the Earth.

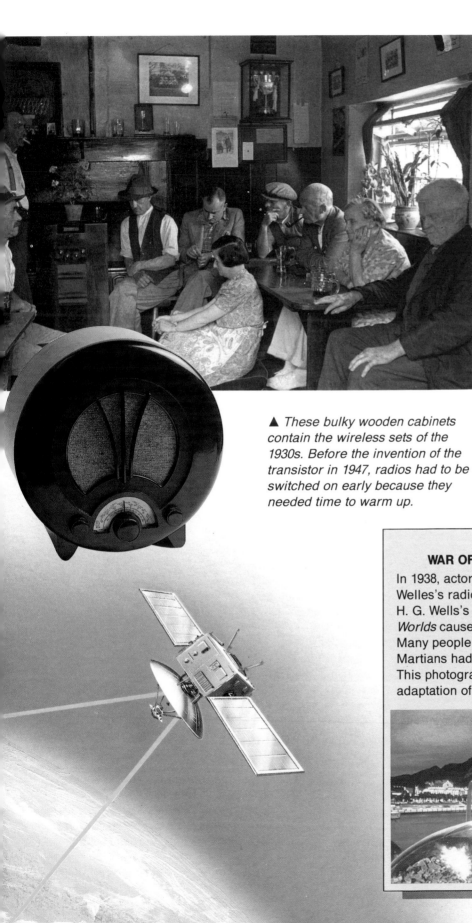

▲ These bulky wooden cabinets contain the wireless sets of the 1930s. Before the invention of the transistor in 1947, radios had to be switched on early because they needed time to warm up.

WAR OF THE WORLDS

In 1938, actor-director Orson Welles's radio broadcast of H. G. Wells's novel *War of the Worlds* caused mass panic. Many people believed that Martians had really landed. This photograph is from the film adaptation of the book.

▲ A cartoonist predicted the invention of portable radios in 1909. It was another 38 years before the transistor radio appeared, and 70 years before the Sony Walkman was invented.

ON TWO WHEELS

Early bicycles had simple wooden frames, no steering, and no pedals. Riders had to scoot along by pushing their feet against the ground.

A German, Baron Karl von Drais von Sauerbrun, solved the problem of steering when he introduced his "draisienne" in 1817. This model was steered by a bar connected to the front wheel.

Those early cyclists must have worn out many pairs of shoes as they scooted along. Relief for sore feet came in 1839 with the invention of pedals by a Scottish blacksmith, Kirkpatrick Macmillan. His bicycle was called a velocipede, and the pedals were connected by rods to the wheels.

One of the most popular bicycles of the last century was the penny-farthing, named after two different-sized British coins of the time. This odd-looking bike had a huge front wheel (to which the pedals were attached) and a tiny back one. The first penny-farthing was built in England in 1870 by James Starley. These bicycles were popular, but they were also dangerous to ride.

This hazard led his nephew John Starley to design the Rover safety bicycle 15 years later. It had spoked wheels of equal size, a chain drive connecting the pedals with the wheels, and solid rubber tires. Bikes were beginning to look like the machines we ride today.

FACT FILE

The first drawing of a bicycle was made three thousand years ago by an Egyptian artist in the Temple of Luxor.

The pneumatic tire was first fitted to a bicycle in 1888 by John Boyd Dunlop. He filled the tire with air to give his invalid son a more comfortable ride.

Leonardo da Vinci sketched a design for a bicycle 500 years ago, but it was never built.

There are more than 200 million bicycles in China.

▶ The invention of the bicycle inspired people to experiment with different designs. One model was 16 feet (5 meters) tall; the penny-farthing (far right) was dangerous to ride and people often fell off.

▲ In the 1920s, sports clothes of all kinds were popular. Dresses for cycling were designed to provide plenty of room for pedaling, while still keeping up a "ladylike" appearance. This poster shows a woman out in the country in 1924.

▲ Steam can be used to power a wide range of machines. This sewing machine is an example.

FACT FILE

The up-and-down movement of a piston is converted into the rotation of a wheel by sun and planet gears. They were invented in 1782 by James Watt.

The largest steam engine ever built was designed by English engineer Matthew Loam in 1849. It was used for a drainage system. Each piston stroke lifted 13,440 gallons (50,875 liters) of water.

In 1884, Charles Parsons built the first practical steam turbine, where the movement of steam is used to rotate vanes attached to a central shaft.

The world's fastest steam car, the *Steamin' Demon*, was built in the U.S. On August 15, 1985, it reached a speed of 145 mph (234 km/h).

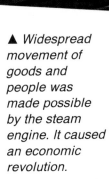

▲ Widespread movement of goods and people was made possible by the steam engine. It caused an economic revolution.

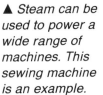

► Today, people drive steam engines for fun. This traction engine rally in England attracts enthusiasts from all over the world.

TRAVEL BY RAIL

The speed of early trains worried members of the British government. They were anxious that passengers traveling faster than 12 miles per hour (19 km/h) might suffocate!

The first steam locomotive, the *New Castle*, was designed by Richard Trevithick. On February 13, 1804, it pulled a loaded coal train for 9 miles (15 kilometres) along a track in southern Wales. Before this, trains were pulled by horses.

By 1821, English engineer George Stephenson had begun to build the first public railroad. His engine, *Locomotion*, carried 400 eager passengers from Stockton to Darlington. By 1829, with the help of his son Robert, he had built an even more powerful engine, *Rocket*, which won a competition for locomotives by reaching the amazing speed of 36 miles per hour (58 kilometers per hour).

Railroads were soon being built all over the world. In 1869, the tracks of the Central Pacific and Union Pacific railroads were linked at Promontory Point, Utah, to form the first transcontinental railroad.

By the 1950s, pollution from steam trains was a serious problem, and diesel and electric engines began to take over.

▶ The Golden Arrow *ran between London and Paris from 1926 to 1972 at speeds almost five times faster than Stephenson's* Rocket. *One of its locomotives,* City of Wells, *now hauls tourists.*

▲ Rocket *was built with 25 heating tubes in its boiler. Later steam locomotives copied this design.*

▼ *The Tay Bridge in Scotland collapsed on December 28, 1879, causing the first serious train accident.*

FACT FILE

Guiding rails for trains were made from wood until 1763. During a slump in the iron industry in England, Richard Reynolds produced the first cast-iron rails.

The world's first subway system was opened in London in 1863.

Air brakes for trains were invented in the U.S. by George Westinghouse in 1869. They used compressed air to clamp brake shoes to the wheels.

The first electric locomotive was developed in Germany by Werner von Siemens and Johann Malske in 1879.

The first diesel locomotive was built in 1912 by the Sulzer Company of Switzerland.

In 1926, the British steam locomotive *Mallard* set a steam rail speed record of 126 mph (203 km/h). The engine suffered slight damage!

In 1964, the first "Bullet" trains hurtled between Osaka and Tokyo in Japan at 130 mph (210 km/h).

Trains that "float" above the track are operated by magnetic levitation (maglev). This system uses magnetic force to move trains along a track which they never actually touch.

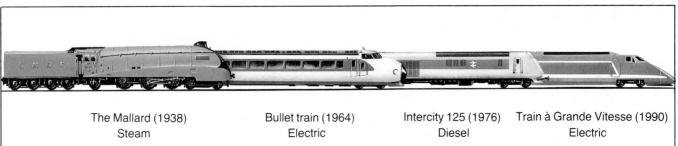

| The Mallard (1938) | Bullet train (1964) | Intercity 125 (1976) | Train à Grande Vitesse (1990) |
| Steam | Electric | Diesel | Electric |

▲ This century has seen an amazing advance in the speed of passenger trains.
The Mallard 126 mph (203 km/h);
Bullet train 130 mph (210 km/h);
Intercity 125 148 mph (238 km/h)
TGV 320 mph (515 km/h).

◄ The French Train à Grande Vitesse, or TGV, is the world's fastest train. It runs on special high-speed tracks and reached 320 mph (515 km/h) during a test run in May, 1990.

THE STORY OF PHOTOGRAPHY

The camera is basically a box with an opening through which light enters. It is focused by a lens onto a light-sensitive film which "captures" the image. Today's cameras work in a fraction of a second, but in 1840 taking a picture was quite an ordeal. Body supports were needed to help keep people still for the time needed to get a clear image.

The first photograph was taken by Frenchman Joseph Niepce in 1826. It shows the view from his window. The exposure (the time the film is shown to the light) lasted for a marathon eight hours. Niepce's breakthrough was the use of a chemical, silver chloride, which was sensitive to light.

A few years later, Louis Daguerre devised the daguerrotype process, which shortened exposure times to just 30 minutes. He discovered by accident that a "hidden" image could be stored on a copper plate coated with silver iodide. The image was then "developed" with mercury vapor and "fixed" with common salt. It was not until 1837, though, that he found a way to stop the image from fading away.

◄ This photograph, which was taken in 1837, is the oldest surviving daguerrotype.

▼ The man having his boots cleaned stood still long enough to become the first person to be photographed. Louis Daguerre took the photograph in 1839.

▼ This photograph of schoolgirl Frances Griffiths and the dancing fairies is a very famous "fake." It was taken in 1917 by Frances's cousin, Elsie Wright.

◄ This is the first camera to be sold to the public. It was introduced in 1839 by Louis Daguerre. The camera had no shutter, and exposures could last up to 40 minutes.

▶ *Hummingbirds can beat their wings more than 50 times a second. This photo of a green-cheeked Amazon hummingbird was taken with a special high-speed camera.*

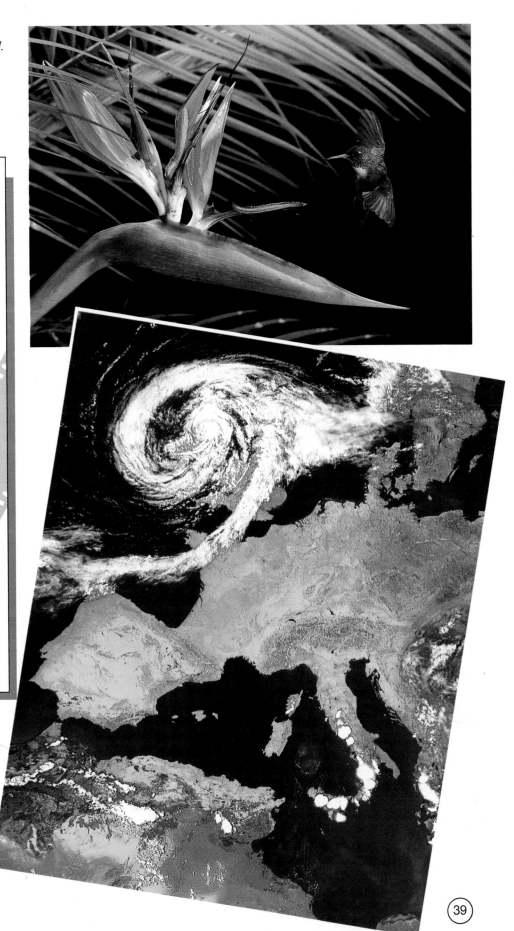

▶ *Satellite photographs can be used to keep an eye on the weather. This picture shows a massive storm system covering most of the British Isles. It was taken on August 6, 1987, by the NOAA-9 weather satellite. These pictures are often used during television weather forecasts.*

39

THE MOVING IMAGE

"You ain't seen nothing yet." When Al Jolson said these words in the 1927 movie *The Jazz Singer*, the audience was astonished. No one had spoken in films before – the "talkies" had arrived.

Early experiments with moving images were made at the end of the last century, but it was a request from a racehorse owner that unwittingly helped the invention of the movies. Photographer Eadweard Muybridge was asked to prove that a galloping horse lifts all of its hoofs off the ground at the same time. He used 12 cameras to produce a set of photographs which he mounted on a revolving disc. As the pictures were projected in quick succession, the horse appeared to move.

On December 28, 1895, the first true movies were screened in public by two French brothers, Louis and Auguste Lumière.

Their camera, which took a reel of film over 45 feet (14 meters) long, projected pictures at 16 frames per second.

Early silent movies had sound "added" by someone playing the organ or piano. In the very early talking pictures, actors mimed, and sound was recorded on a disc and played separately.

▼ *A movie camera and microphone are set up to record. The lion became the trademark of MGM films.*

▶ *The Lumière's cinematograph was a combined camera, printer, and projector.*

▶ *The praxinoscope projected a sequence of drawn pictures onto a screen. A candle provided the light. This device was invented in France by Emile Reynaud and became a popular toy in the late 1800s.*

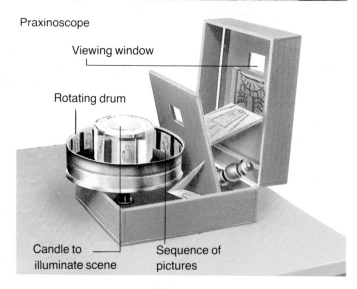

Praxinoscope

Viewing window

Rotating drum

Candle to illuminate scene

Sequence of pictures

▶ The film King Kong *was made in 1933. It used a small-scale model of New York to make the gorilla appear supersized.*

▲ *Animated films use 24 images every second. This is artwork used for Walt Disney's film* Fantasia.

▶ *Today, cameras are small enough to be taken anywhere on location. These operators are filming* Baron von Munchausen.

Flick through the pages of this book, and the man, drawn after photographs by Eadweard Muybridge, appears to move. This shows how moving pictures work.

TELEVISION

There are 200 million television sets in the U.S. – nearly one for every person. The success of television owes much to a Scot, John Logie Baird, who trained as an engineer but then tried to make a fortune making artificial diamonds and "self-warming" socks.

After these ideas failed, Baird began his experiments with television. The idea was to send a picture by radio. In 1924, using scrap-yard junk held together with glue and string, a hatbox, and some knitting needles, he made a machine which worked.

Meanwhile in the U.S., the Russian-born inventor Vladimir Zworykin was working on a different system. Baird's television used spinning disks to record and display the pictures, but Zworykin's system was all electronic. During the 1920s, Zworykin perfected an electronic camera, the iconoscope.

When public broadcasting of TV began, the electronic system was adopted. The picture is produced when a beam of electrons hits a screen covered with special dots. When electrons hit the dots, they give off light. This device is called a cathode-ray tube.

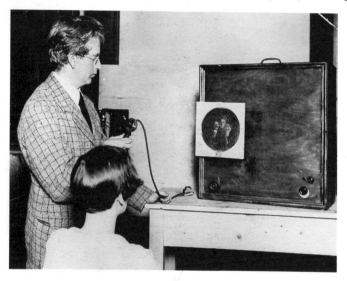

▲ The first practical television was Baird's "Televisor," demonstrated in 1926. The round screen shows Baird watching while his assistant holds up two dolls.

In the 1930s, British television ▲ sets looked like this. The tiny screen showed black-and-white pictures.

FACT FILE

In 1884, German engineer Paul Nipkow built an "electric" telescope which sent an exact image of an object along a wire and projected it onto a screen.

The first outside broadcast was made in London in 1937 using a portable transmitter.

All modern TV works in the same way. Light from a scene is scanned by a camera and "translated" into electronic signals which are sent into the atmosphere. They are picked up by a receiver and put back together again in the TV set to re-create the picture.

Color television only has three colors – the picture is made up of tiny dots that glow red, blue, and green. The eye and brain are tricked into believing they can see the whole color range.

► In the U.S., a television picture is made up of 525 lines. British televisions use 625 lines. Engineers are working on a new system called High Definition Television. It will have as many as 1,250 lines, to give a much sharper picture.

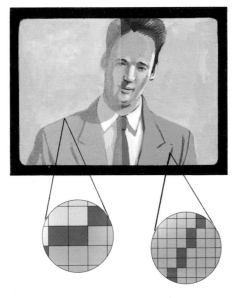

► Television sets are becoming smaller every year. The first pocket television was developed by Sir Clive Sinclair in 1981, but this wristwatch television is even smaller.

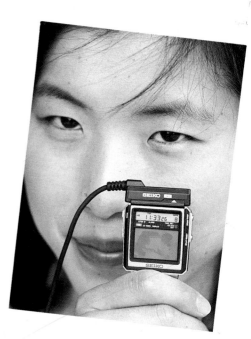

▼ This is the view from the newsreader's desk. The screen in front of her shows last-minute changes. Camera 1 shows the script which can be read while facing the camera.

◄ This is the control room of a television studio. The screens show different camera angles, and the director chooses the image to be broadcast.

▲ The newsreader faces an automatic control camera to read the news. An autocue above the camera magnifies the script for her to read.

THE TELEPHONE LINK

"Come here, Watson, I want you," were the first words ever spoken over the telephone. It was March 1876, and Alexander Graham Bell had accidentally spilled acid on his clothes. Bell's voice was heard by his assistant, Thomas Watson, who was working in another room. Alexander Graham Bell's invention was working at last.

Bell was born in Scotland but later moved to the United States. His mother was deaf, and his father taught deaf children, as Bell later would himself. Through his work in speech and sound, Bell came to believe that sound could be changed into an electric current, which could then pass along a wire and be changed back into sound again. This inspired him to invent the telephone.

There are now more than 500 million telephones in the world, and two fifths of them are in the U.S. The Pentagon, in Washington, D.C., has the world's largest switchboard, handling 200,000 calls a day.

Most telephones now have push buttons instead of a circular dial. Some telephones are cordless and can be carried anywhere, while others are installed in cars. These kinds of phones use radio waves to link up with the phone cable system.

▲ *Imagine trying to find a crossed line here. This telegraph pole in Philadelphia, photographed in 1909, carried a separate wire for each telephone. Modern technology lets hundreds of conversations travel along the same pair of wires or fiber-optic cables.*

◄ *This "candlestick" telephone may look like an antique, but 100 years ago it was the latest in high technology.*

ALEXANDER GRAHAM BELL

1847: Born on March 3, in Edinburgh, Scotland.

1876: Achieved first transmission of speech by telephone.

1890: Founded the American Association to Promote Teaching of Speech to the Deaf.

1915: Opened first transcontinental telephone line, between New York and San Francisco.

1922: Died on August 2.

▲ Breaking down in the desert can be very dangerous. Luckily, this Saudi Arabian driver is able to call for help on a solar-powered radiophone. Many international calls are sent via satellites in space, which can carry a staggering 50,000 calls at the same time.

◄ This 1899 picture shows the kind of videophone which people thought would be in use by the year 2000. A more likely development by the beginning of the next century is the use of computers to translate telephone messages from one language into another.

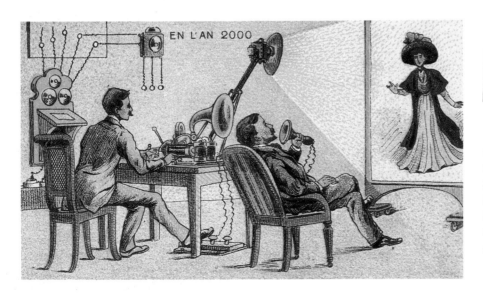

X-RAYS

X-rays are invisible waves of energy. They can travel easily through matter such as skin or cardboard, but may be absorbed by heavier matter such as metal or bones.

These electromagnetic waves were discovered by accident in 1895 by German physicist Wilhelm Roentgen. He had been studying how electricity passes through certain gases. For his experiment he was using a gas-filled tube wrapped in cardboard so that no light could get out. Roentgen noticed that some chemicals on the other side of the room were glowing in the dark. When he switched off the electricity in the tube, the chemicals stopped glowing.

He realized that some type of ray must be coming out of the tube, passing through the cardboard, and making the chemicals glow. Roentgen spent the next six weeks studying the mysterious rays, which he named X-rays. Before long, he understood that they could be used to detect broken bones and other ailments within the body.

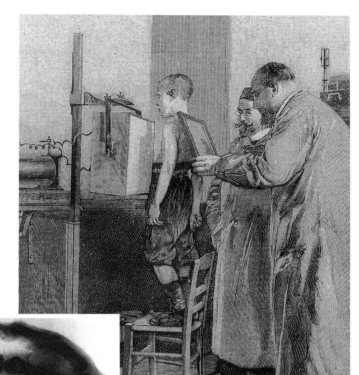

▶ Roentgen began using X-rays within a few months of their discovery. This child is having an X-ray taken of his chest.

▼ The first X-ray ever taken shows Bertha Roentgen's hand. You can see that she was wearing a wedding ring.

▶ X-rays can be dangerous if they are not used carefully. Very large doses can cause cancer. The first people to use X-rays did not realize the dangers, but by 1909, protective clothing like this was being worn.

FACT FILE

Wilhelm Roentgen was awarded the first ever Nobel Prize for Physics in 1901 for his discovery of X-rays. The exact nature of the rays was identified by Max von Laue in 1912.

X-rays were used in a hospital in New Hampshire only two months after they were discovered. The doctors used them to look at a broken bone.

X-rays from space were discovered by scientists at White Sands, New Mexico, in 1948. They launched an X-ray detector aboard a captured German V2 missile.

X-rays have been used to produce changes in the cell structure of a variety of barley that enable it to grow in poor soils.

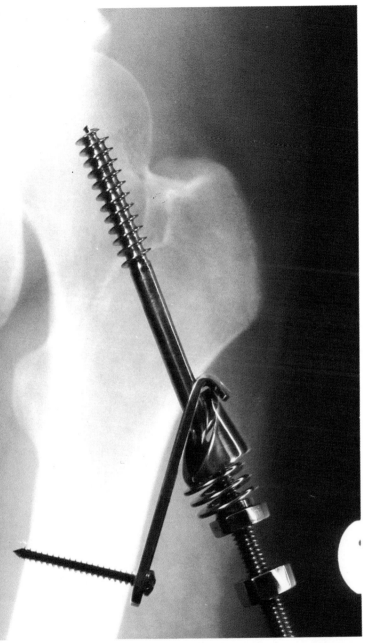

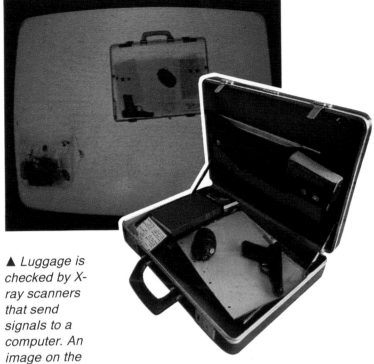

▲ Luggage is checked by X-ray scanners that send signals to a computer. An image on the computer screen shows what is in the case.

◀ Broken bones sometimes need to be screwed together to help them heal. This X-ray picture shows a fractured hip bone which has been repaired with a screw.

▼ Computerized Axial Tomographic (CAT) scanners can be used to see inside the brain. They were invented by the British physicist Godfrey Hounsfield in 1971. Hounsfield shared the Nobel Prize for Medicine in 1979.

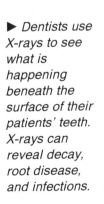

▶ Dentists use X-rays to see what is happening beneath the surface of their patients' teeth. X-rays can reveal decay, root disease, and infections.

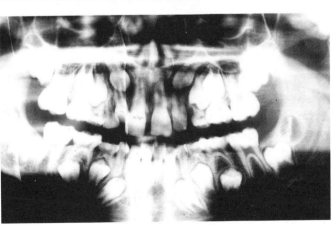

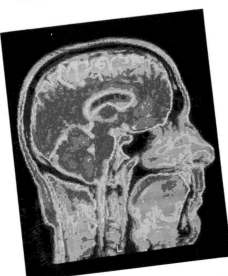

THE SOUND OF MUSIC

Like all sound, music is made when something vibrates. This vibration can be created by blowing air inside a tube, by plucking a length of string or "stroking" it with a bow, or by hitting a piece of wood, metal, or skin stretched over a drum.

The ancient Egyptians were great music-makers and played instruments similar to the oboe, flute, and trumpet of today. Over the centuries, music-makers have invented different ways of making the sound of music sweeter, purer, and more varied. By the seventeenth century, popular instruments included the harp, lute, flute, harpsichord, and organ.

Modern music really began with the invention of the piano, the "harpsichord with hammers," in the early eighteenth century. The strings in a harpsichord are plucked, but for the piano, Italian Bartolomeo Cristofori invented a way of hitting each string which allowed the loudness of the sound to be controlled by how hard the key was pressed – impossible with the harpsichord.

Today, computerized synthesizers can mimic other instruments, and even make sounds that have never been heard before.

▶ *Lutes and harps have been played for over 4,000 years. A modern harp has 46 strings of different lengths. Harps were popular instruments during the 16th century.*

▼ *The earliest horns were, as their name suggests, animal horns. People blew through them to produce musical notes. During the 18th century, spiral horns were produced in France. The modern French horn was designed during the 1800s. It has three valves that alter the length of tubing and enable a range of different notes to be played.*

BOY WONDER
Wolfgang Amadeus Mozart showed astonishing musical talent. He gave public performances on the harpsichord at the age of six, wrote his first symphony before he was ten and his first opera when he was twelve. He died, aged thirty five, after composing more than 600 major works.

◀ There are usually six double basses in an orchestra. This is the world's biggest double bass. Imagine trying to get it in a car!

▲ This one-man band is performing on Fifth Avenue, New York, in 1980.

▼ Modern musicians play some strange instruments. This globe plays a different note as each color is touched.

FACT FILE

The shofar, made from a ram's horn, has been used in Jewish religious ceremonies throughout history.

The world's most valuable violins are those produced by Italian violin-maker Antonio Stradivari, between 1666 and 1737. A Stradivarius has such a fine tone because of the thickness of the wood and its minute pores, in which air vibrates, and the formula of the deep-colored varnish.

The French horn's 11 feet (3.3 meters) of tubing are curled up to make it easy to carry.

A German piano tuner named C. F. L. Buschmann wanted an instrument that would help him tune pianos – the result, in 1821, was the invention of the harmonica.

In trying to improve the clarinet, Belgian Adolphe Sax invented the saxophone. The year was 1846.

In 1954, Robert Moog began the design of an electronic instrument which he called a synthesizer. Computerized synthesizers are now used to produce sounds that have never been heard before.

FORWARD ON FOUR WHEELS

In 1769, Nicholas Cugnot crashed his steam carriage into a wall. Cugnot's journey lasted just twenty minutes, but his carriage was the world's first mechanically propelled road vehicle.

The first practical motorcar was built by German engineer Karl Benz in 1885. It had three wheels and a gasoline engine which was connected to the rear axle by a leather belt. The Motorwagen, as the car was called, had a top speed of 10 miles per hour (16 km/h). Another German, Gottlieb Daimler, built the first four-wheeled model in 1886.

The first cars were made by hand and were very expensive.

Cars became available to ordinary people thanks to the inventiveness of Henry Ford. His Model T was introduced in 1908 and was the first mass-produced car. Model T's were built on an assembly line and moved from one group of workers to the next. By carefully timing each

worker's part in the assembly, a car chassis could be put together in 1 hour 33 minutes, compared to a previous best of over 12 hours. More than 15 million Model T's, nicknamed "Tin Lizzies," were sold between 1908 and 1927.

◄ Gottlieb Daimler's 1886 Daimler-Wagen was the first four-wheeled car. Daimler and Benz were great rivals and often argued about who had built the first car.

▼ This wooden-bodied amphibious car is designed to travel on land and in the water.

FACT FILE

1885: Karl Benz produced the first gasoline-driven car.

1891: In France, René Panhard and Emile Levassor built the first car to have its engine at the front.

1902: Louis Renault produced a simple but effective drum brake that was soon developed for use on most automobiles.

1908: Henry Ford introduced the Model T. It was only offered in black, because this paint dried more quickly.

1936: The Volkswagen Beetle was devised by Ferdinand Porsche in Germany.

1959: Sir Alec Issigonis launched the first Mini in Britain. The engine was installed sideways in the small, but revolutionary, car. More than five million were sold.

▼ On October 4, 1983, British driver Richard Noble set a new land speed record when his jet-powered car, Thrust 2, traveled at 633 mph (1,019 km/h) across the Black Rock Desert in Nevada.

◄ Formula One racing cars have special airfoils. These hold the cars down on the track as they travel at speeds up to 200 mph (320 km/h). This is the reverse action of the airfoil on a plane's wing which lifts it off the ground.

▼ "Stretch" limousines are popular, but this one takes things rather too far. The Cadillac Eldorado 1982 is 71 ft 11 in (22 meters) long, has 18 wheels, and weighs more than 7 tons. It has a swimming pool, television, VCR, three telephones, and enough space for twenty people.

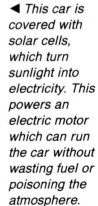

◄ This car is covered with solar cells, which turn sunlight into electricity. This powers an electric motor which can run the car without wasting fuel or poisoning the atmosphere.

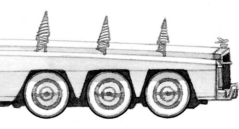

EARLY FLIGHT

"Beware – flying sheep!" That warning could have been used in Paris, France, in 1783. Joseph Montgolfier and his brother Etienne were testing their new hot-air balloon. The first passengers were a sheep, a rooster, and a duck. On November 21, the balloon took to the skies again, this time carrying Jean Pilatre de Rozier and the Marquis d'Arlandes; the first men to fly.

Yet balloon passengers could only travel where the wind took them. The next step in the quest for the skies, to build a craft with a steering mechanism, was made by Englishman Sir George Cayley. He built a model glider (a plane with no engine) in 1803 and spent the next 50 years perfecting the design. By the time he had built a full-sized version in 1853, he was too old to fly. He sent his terrified coach driver up in the glider instead.

Another 50 years passed before the first airplane, powered by an engine, took to the air. This was the *Flyer*, built in the U.S. by Wilbur Wright and his brother, Orville. On December 17, 1903, Orville piloted the machine for 120 feet (36.5 meters) at Kitty Hawk, North Carolina. The flight lasted just 12 seconds and was watched by Wilbur Wright, four men, and a boy.

▼ *Following their successful flight in 1903, the Wright brothers made headline news around the world. Wilbur Wright took the* Flyer *to France in 1908.*

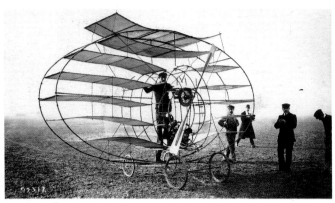

▲ *Some early designs for aircraft looked very strange. One craft was fitted with multiple wings . . .*

◄ *. . . another had a second pair of wheels on top so that it could land upside down!*

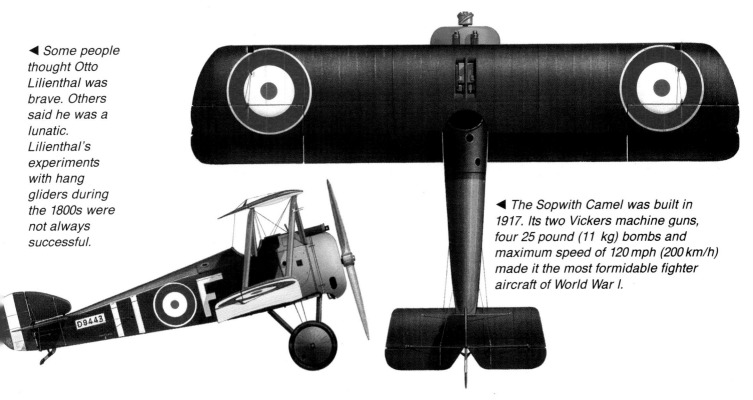

◀ Some people thought Otto Lilienthal was brave. Others said he was a lunatic. Lilienthal's experiments with hang gliders during the 1800s were not always successful.

◀ The Sopwith Camel was built in 1917. Its two Vickers machine guns, four 25 pound (11 kg) bombs and maximum speed of 120 mph (200 km/h) made it the most formidable fighter aircraft of World War I.

AIR MAIL.

◀ At the beginning of this century, letters to other parts of the world had to be sent by sea. This airmail letter was sent in 1928 and carries a tribute to Charles Lindbergh's solo flight across the Atlantic Ocean.

▶ A total of 22,759 Supermarine Spitfires were built during World War II. They played an important role in the Battle of Britain.

FACT FILE

1783: Montgolfier brothers' balloon carried the first people to fly.

1852: Frenchman Henri Giffard made the first flight in a mechanically propelled airship.

1853: Sir George Cayley's glider made a successful flight.

1900: Prototype Zeppelin airship flew for the first time.

1909: Frenchman Louis Blériot thrilled the world when he flew across the Channel from England to France.

1919: John Alcock and Arthur Brown made the first nonstop flight across the Atlantic.

1930: Amy Johnson became the first woman to fly solo from Britain to Australia in 19 days.

INTO THE JET AGE

Jet planes can travel faster than a bullet and twice the speed of sound. These amazing speeds are reached by using jet engines, which burn fuel with oxygen to produce gases that are expelled so fast, the force pushes the plane forward.

The jet engine was patented in 1930 by British aviator Frank Whittle. He had entered the Royal Air Force as a boy apprentice, and he invented the jet engine while he was still a student. The first jet to take off using Whittle's engine was the Gloster E28/29 in 1941, and by 1945, the Gloster Meteor jet had gone into action in World War II.

After the war, air travel opened up the world to the public, and the race for bigger, faster jets began. However, since the early 1940s, aviators had been trying to travel faster than the speed of sound, or 660 miles per hour (1,062 km/h).

American pilot Chuck Yeager achieved this speed in 1947 in a rocket-powered plane, the Bell X-1. However, it was not until 1969 that the Anglo-French jet Concorde took to the skies and broke the sound barrier.

Today, planes such as the Boeing 747 can carry 500 passengers to the other side of the world in less than 24 hours. The American X-30 aerospace plane, due to fly during the 1990s, will zoom from Britain to Australia, or from the United States to Japan, in less than two hours.

▲ *Helicopters are called VTOL craft, which stands for Vertical Take Off and Landing. The blades push air under the helicopter, as a wing does with an airplane. Helicopters can fly backward and forward, or hover. They need very little space to take off or land, and can carry very heavy objects, even houses!*

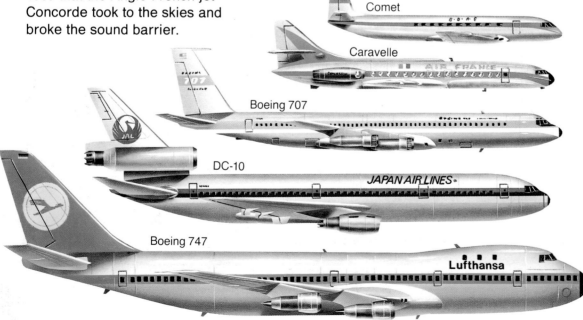

Comparative size of jets

Comet

Caravelle

Boeing 707

DC-10

Boeing 747

◄ *The size of jet airliners increased steadily throughout the 1950s and 60s. The Comet, which entered service in 1952, was the world's first passenger jet. The Boeing 747 first flew in 1969 and is still the world's largest airplane.*

Shuttle enters orbit

External tank is
jettisoned

Solid
rocket
boosters
separate

Launch

◄ The space shuttle is the world's most complicated flying machine. A typical orbit places it 250 miles (400 km) above the Earth, traveling at 16,500 mph (26,500 km/h). During re-entry through the atmosphere, friction heats the outside of the shuttle to 2,750°F (1,510°C).

FACT FILE

1930: Frank Whittle patented the jet engine.

1939: Igor Sikorsky's VS-300, the first modern helicopter, took to the air.

1939: The first turbojet aircraft, the German Heinkel He-178, was built.

1953: Rolls Royce's "Flying Bedstead" made its first attempt at a vertical takeoff.

1976: Concorde, traveling at speeds up to 1,300 mph (2,090 km/h) started a regular passenger service.

▲ The world air-speed record is held by the Lockheed SR-71 Blackbird. The record stands at 2,193 mph (3,529 km/h), set on July 28, 1976.

▲ The first nonstop flight around the world without refueling was made in 1986 by Dick Rutan and Jeanna Yeager.

55

TIME TRAVEL

By the time he was twelve years old, Albert Einstein had already decided to devote himself to solving the "riddle of the huge world." As a young man, he had an amazing thought. "What would it be like to travel on a beam of light?"

This question led Einstein to his special theory of relativity, which included the notion that nothing can travel faster than light. This meant that everything else in the universe must be changeable, including time and movement, and that time passes more slowly the faster you are moving.

In 1971, two American scientists proved Einstein right.

They took accurate clocks around the Earth on jet aircraft and showed that they went 59 thousand millionths of a second slower than clocks on the ground!

The special theory of relativity also concerned energy and the way that it is locked into the atoms that make up our universe. This part of the theory led other scientists to develop the atomic bomb.

Another idea that became part of Einstein's "general theory," was that gravity could bend light. Astronomers now believe that some objects have such strong gravity that they even "capture" light. These are called black holes.

ALBERT EINSTEIN
1879: Born in Ulm, Germany, March 14.
1905: Special relativity theory.
1915: General relativity theory.
1921: Won Nobel Prize for Physics.
1933: Moved to U.S.
1939: Began work on atom bomb.
1955: Died on April 18.

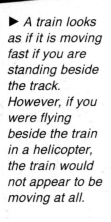

◀ *Einstein stated that all motion is relative. We can never measure how fast we are traveling; we can only tell how fast we are moving in relation to something else. People on a train are moving very fast in relation to the countryside around them, but they are not moving at all in relation to each other.*

▶ *A train looks as if it is moving fast if you are standing beside the track. However, if you were flying beside the train in a helicopter, the train would not appear to be moving at all.*

▼ *Einstein's equation shows that the Energy (E) of a body equals its mass (m) times the speed of light (c) squared. This predicted the energy of the atom bomb.*

▼ *Einstein proposed many theories that seemed strange to people, but experiments have since proved his theories true. He stated that nothing can travel faster than the speed of light – 186,000 miles per second (300,000 km/sec). A light beam can reach the Moon from Earth in 1.3 seconds. Here are examples of how long it would take some animals and vehicles to get there.*

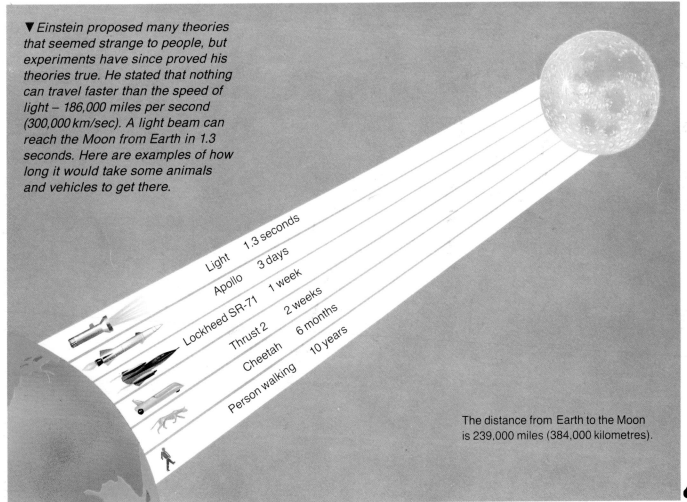

Light   1.3 seconds
Apollo   3 days
Lockheed SR-71   1 week
Thrust 2   2 weeks
Cheetah   6 months
Person walking   10 years

The distance from Earth to the Moon is 239,000 miles (384,000 kilometres).

NUCLEAR POWER

Everything that exists in the universe is made of atoms. At the center of each atom is the nucleus, which contains tightly packed, minute particles called protons and neutrons. If the nucleus is split, huge amounts of energy are suddenly released. If this happens quickly, it produces a nuclear explosion. If the energy is released slowly, it can be used to generate electricity.

The neutrons themselves play a part in this. When an atom of uranium-235 (a type of uranium with an especially active nucleus) is bombarded by neutrons, the nucleus splits and releases not just energy, but also more neutrons. These neutrons collide with other nuclei and make them split, producing still more neutrons. This process is called a chain reaction. Nuclear power stations operate by keeping a chain reaction going inside a reactor.

In 1939, German scientist Otto Hahn made a uranium-235 nucleus split. Three years later, Italian physicist Enrico Fermi built the first nuclear reactor.

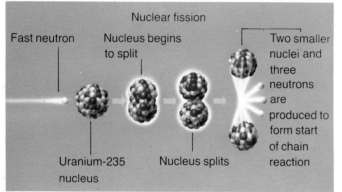

Nuclear fission

Fast neutron

Nucleus begins to split

Two smaller nuclei and three neutrons are produced to form start of chain reaction

Uranium-235 nucleus

Nucleus splits

◀ *The process by which the nucleus of an atom splits into two or more pieces is called nuclear fission. Splitting the nucleus this way releases a lot of energy.*

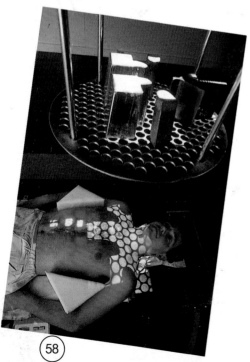

▼ *Doctors can use radiation from nuclear reactions to treat cancer in radiotherapy. This radiation is being aimed at the bright patches on the patient's chest.*

► *Nuclear submarines can remain submerged for much longer than conventional submarines. The first nuclear submarine was the U.S.S. Nautilus, which was launched by the navy on January 21, 1954. Nautilus became the first submarine to surface at the North Pole, on August 3, 1958.*

◄ *Nuclear power stations use the heat produced by nuclear reactions to boil water. The water turns to steam and drives turbines which generate electricity. The world's first nuclear power station was the EBR-1 in Idaho, which opened on December 20, 1951.*

► LASER LIGHT

When you shine a flashlight, the beam of light spreads out and covers a large area. Do the same with a laser, and the beam produces a tiny, bright point.

This is because ordinary light is a mixture of different colors, radiating in all directions, whereas laser light has just one pure color and always travels in the same direction, so its beam is extremely bright.

The theory of the laser was first suggested by Albert Einstein in 1917, but more than 40 years passed before one was built. Two American scientists, Charles Townes and Arthur Schawlow, explained how a laser could be built in 1958. However, the first working laser was built in 1960 by Theodore Maiman. His laser used a crystal of synthetic ruby to produce light that was ten million times more powerful than sunlight.

Today, lasers have many different uses. Surgeons can use lasers to perform delicate operations. The laser can also be used in industry for cutting and welding metal. On a compact disc, information is stored in the form of microscopic pits which can be "read" by a laser beam in the compact-disc player.

► *The intense power of a laser can be used in factories for cutting and drilling. This laser is cutting a shape from a stack of cloth.*

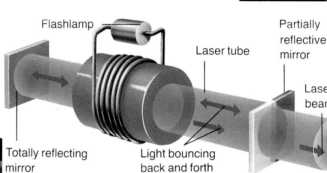

Flashlamp

Partially reflective mirror

Laser tube

Laser beam

Totally reflecting mirror

Light bouncing back and forth

◄ *A burst of energy from the flashlamp makes atoms in the laser tube give off light. This gets stronger as it bounces backward and forward.*

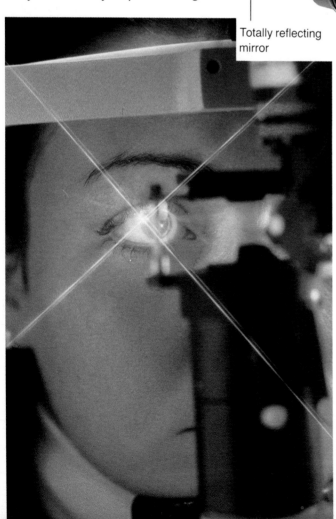

◄ *Surgeons can use lasers for delicate eye operations. A laser can "weld" together damaged tissue at the back of the eye.*

FACT FILE

LASER stands for Light Amplification by Stimulated Emission of Radiation.

Lasers have been used to measure the distance from the Earth to the Moon to the nearest 2 inches (5 cm).

In crime detection, lasers can be used to reveal fingerprints left on a surface for 40 years.

Hungarian scientist Dennis Gabor developed the idea of the hologram in 1947. The name, *hologram*, is made of the Greek words *holos* (whole) and *gramma* (message), and means "the whole message."

► Lasers can produce some spectacular effects. The Empire State Building in New York City was lit with lasers to celebrate its fiftieth anniversary.

► American artist Rick Silbermann produced this intriguing image of a champagne glass. A picture of the lower part of the glass has been combined with a hologram of the whole glass before it was broken.

◄ Holograms are special types of photographs made by using a laser. A hologram image is three-dimensional, so the object in the picture looks solid. If you look at a hologram from different positions, you will see different views of the same object. This hologram is at the Museum of La Villette in Paris.

THE COMPUTER AGE

Computers were invented to speed up doing arithmetic. Charles Babbage, the man who first dreamed up the idea, was born some 200 years ago in 1792. Using cogs and gears, he made a mechanical calculator that could solve complicated math problems.

Next, Babbage designed an "analytical engine," which could read math problems from punched cards and then work out the answers. Instructions for the machine were written by Countess Ada Lovelace, daughter of the poet Lord Byron; she thus became the world's first computer programmer.

Sadly for Babbage, his ideas were ahead of his time. The technology of the 1830s was not advanced enough to construct the analytical engine, and it was never built. Luckily, Babbage's notes were not destroyed, and the forgotten design was rediscovered by chance in 1937.

After Babbage, little advance was made for a century. Real progress came in the 1940s, when computers were made with electronic valves.

▲ Charles Babbage's dream in the 1830s was the "analytical engine," an early form of computer. The program would have been fed in on punched cards, and the machine would have been powered by a steam engine.

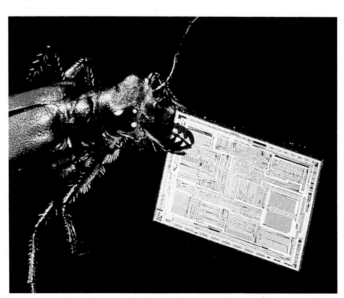

► Insects can be tiny, but integrated circuits are even smaller. This circuit contains all the electronics for a desktop computer.

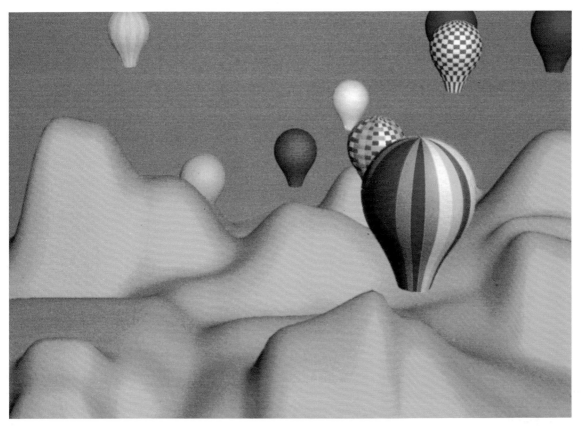

◀ The Cray 2 supercomputer can perform 1,600 million operations every second. It can create three-dimensional scenes, like this landscape with hot-air balloons.

◀ Flight simulators help pilots learn to fly. The view the pilot sees from the cockpit is produced and controlled by a computer.

▶ In the future, cars will have computers to help drivers find their route and to "read" the condition of the road ahead.

TECHNOLOGY IN THE HOME

One hundred years ago, homes were heated by coal or wood fires, and lit by gas lamps. Cleaning the house, washing clothes, and preparing food were all done by hand.

At the turn of the century a new power source – electricity – changed all that forever. Although the first power stations were built during the 1880s, most homes did not have electricity until well into the twentieth century.

In 1913, the first domestic refrigerator went on sale in Chicago. This machine used an electric motor, instead of a small steam engine, to reduce the temperature inside the cabinet.

Then, in 1924, Clarence Birdseye invented modern frozen foods. He had been living in Canada, where he watched the Inuits preserving meat and fish by hanging them outside in the cold. Months later they would bring the food inside, thaw it out, and then cook the still fresh meat. Birdseye returned to the U.S., where his frozen foods soon became a huge success.

Electric gadgets such as pop-up toasters, blenders, and kettles started to appear in the 1920s. Today, refrigerators automatically defrost, microchips control a washing-machine cycle, and radio (micro) waves cook our food.

▲ *Early vacuum cleaners were operated by hand. In 1901, Hubert Booth invented an electric vacuum cleaner. Murray Spengler improved the design and then sold the rights to William Hoover.*

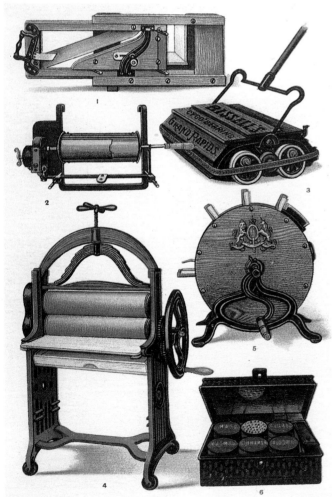

◄ *These items look as though they belong in a museum, but in 1907 they were the latest in high technology.*
1 Bread cutter
2 Coffee roaster
3 Carpet sweeper
4 Wringer and
*   mangle*
5 Knife cleaner
6 Spice box

FACT FILE

The first electric iron was invented by Henry W. Seeley in 1882, but he could not sell any of his irons, because homes were not yet wired up for electricity.

In 1901, Scotsman Hubert Booth invented an electric machine that sucked in dust. The machine was so big that it had to be pulled from house to house by horses.

In 1906, the term air-conditioning was used for the first time by Stuart Crawer. He combined his dust filter with W. H. Carrier's device for cooling air in buildings.

The first microwave oven was patented by the Raytheon Corporation of America in 1953.

▲ Hand-operated washing machines were produced during the 19th century. Alva Fisher designed the first electric washing machine in 1901.

▲ This picture shows a typical kitchen of 1936. Electric lights, vinyl flooring, and fitted units made kitchens brighter and more hygienic places to work.

▼ This is the control center of a prototype computerized house in Dallas, Texas. Computers control all the household systems, including heating, lighting, air-conditioning, and even burglar alarms.

▲ This tea-maker was produced during the early 1900s. The three teapots were kept warm by water heated by a gas burner

MAKING LIFE EASIER

Since history began, people have been working on inventions to make every aspect of life better and easier for all. Not least of these inventions are those that involve the body itself, which may be born with defects or need "repairs" as it ages.

By the thirteenth century, eyeglasses that used lenses to correct poor sight were being worn in China and in Europe. In 1784, Benjamin Franklin discovered how to correct the vision of someone who was both nearsighted and farsighted by inventing the bifocal. Two separate lenses for each eye were wired together in regular spectacle frames.

People who do not like wearing glasses have an alternative – contact lenses. First invented in 1887, they did not become a practical possibility until 1948, when they were made of plastic. The lens is incredibly simple. It floats on the tears naturally produced in the eye.

Another simple invention was the safety razor. King Camp Gillette made his fortune with this invention, which consisted of a two-sided disposable blade, housed in a screw-closed metal case.

◄ *The modern elevator was invented in the U.S. by Elisha Otis in the 1850s. Otis installed the first public elevator in New York on March 23, 1857. More unusual models included this elevator that used heavy containers of water to lift the "cage" up and down.*

◄ *The development of modern building materials has enabled architects to design glass-sided elevators that glide smoothly up and down. The fastest elevator in operation today is in Tokyo. It can travel 1,968 feet (600 meters) in just one minute.*

◀ This is Britain's first laundromat, which opened in London in 1949 for a six-month trial. The first laundromat was opened at Fort Worth, Texas, in 1934, by J. F. Cantrell.

▼ The first industrial robot was produced in the U.S. by Unimation Co., in 1962. This robot nurse is out for a walk in the park.

▶ False teeth were once made from animal bones, which turned brown and smelly. Modern plastic teeth do not have such problems.

THE SPACE RACE

For years, scientists and writers had dreamed of traveling to the Moon. This dream became real, thanks to the pioneering work of American scientist Dr. Robert Goddard. Early rockets used solid fuel, but had very little power. In 1926, Goddard launched the first liquid-fueled rocket, which rose 40 feet (12 meters) into the air before landing in his aunt's garden.

This early setback did not deter him from continuing his experiments with liquid fuel. He finally designed a rocket that rose 7,300 feet (2,225 meters) into the sky, thus paving the way for modern rocketry.

Meanwhile, in Germany, Wernher von Braun was developing the V2 rocket which was used against Britain in World War II. "I designed the rocket to blaze the trail to other planets, not to destroy our own," Braun said. He escaped to the United States in the hope of fulfilling that dream.

Braun developed a rocket with three separate stages. His *Saturn 5* had a tail section that launched the rocket, then fell away; a middle section that drove the rocket higher; and a third section which pushed the Apollo capsule out of Earth's orbit and on toward the Moon.

◄ *The space shuttle is the world's first reusable spacecraft. Only the large fuel tank is discarded. The two solid rocket boosters burn for two minutes and then parachute into the ocean to be used again.*

FACT FILE

To reach outer space, rockets must attain a speed of at least 17,000 mph (27,400 km/h).

The first unmanned satellite was *Sputnik I*, launched by the Russians in 1957.

On July 20, 1969, Neil Armstrong became the first person to set foot on the Moon.

Two spiders, Anita and Arabella, were taken into space to see if they could spin a web in zero gravity.

The space shuttle, used mainly to launch satellites, can carry loads of up to 30 tons.

Voyager 2 **carries recordings** of a baby crying, whale sounds, and human voices.

► *American astronaut Rhea Seddon during her mission aboard the shuttle* Discovery *in April, 1985.*

◄ *Drinks must have special containers to prevent droplets from floating around in space. These Coke cans were designed to be used aboard the space shuttle.*

▲ American astronaut Bruce McCandless was the first person to walk in space without a rope connecting him to the spacecraft. Here he is flying in the Manned Maneuvering Unit, or MMU, which enabled him to move around by operating nitrogen gas thrusters.

▶ Lunar Rovers were used during the last three Apollo missions to the Moon. This is the Apollo 17 Rover which was left behind on the Moon, after being driven for 22 miles (35 km).

INDEX

BIBLIOGRAPHY

Music An Illustrated Encyclopedia, Ardley, N., Hamlyn Publishing, Middlesex, UK, 1986
The Usborne Book of How Things Work, Bramwell, M. and Mostyn, D., Usborne Publishing Ltd, London, 1984
The Usborne Science Encyclopedia, Craig, A. and Rosney, C., Usborne Publishing Ltd, London, 1988
The Macmillan Book of How Things Work, Fulsom, M. and M., Macmillan Publishing Co., New York, 1987
Acorn Illustrated Dictionary for Young Computer Users, Goodman, A. and Tregeas T., Cambridge University Press, Cambridge, UK, 1986
The Young Scientist Book of Jets, Hewish, M., Usborne Publishing Ltd, London, Rev. Ed. 1982
Conquest of the Air, Jefferies, D., Franklin Watts, London and New York, 1990.
Pedal Power – The Story of Bicycles, Top Gear – The Story of the Automobile, Jefferies, D. and Lafferty, P., Franklin Watts, London and New York, 1990
The Computer Revolution, Jeremiah, D., Macmillan Children's Books, London, 1983
The Big Book of Space, Kerrod, R., Hamlyn Publishing Group Ltd, London, 1988
Usborne Guide to Films and Special Effects, Meredith, S. and Mottram, P., Usborne Publishing Ltd, London, 1984
The Usborne Book of Space Facts, 1987, *The Usborne Illustrated Dictionary of Invention and Discovery,* 1986, Reid, S., Usborne Publishing Ltd, London
Cambridge Illustrated Dictionary for Young Scientists, Stone, J., Cambridge University Press, Cambridge, UK, 1985
Electricity and Magnetism 1990, *Structures and Materials,* 1990, Whyman, K., Franklin Watts, London